W9-BPK-736

One Big Pair of

LAURA
GEHL
WROTE THE
WORDS

UNDERWEAR

XL

TOM
LICHTENHELD
MADE THE
PICTURES

Beach
Lane
Books

NEW YORK
LONDON
TORONTO
SYDNEY
NEW DELHI

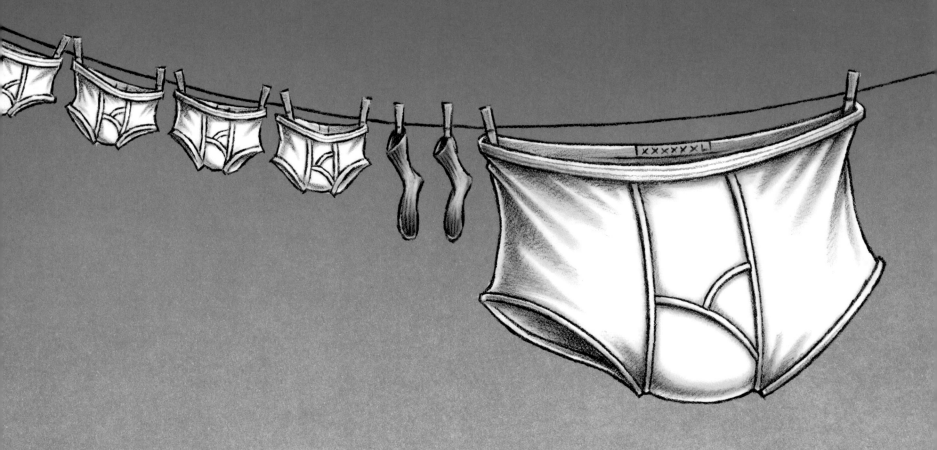

ONE big pair of underwear.

TWO brown bears who hate to share.

ONE bear wears the underwear.

ONE bear cries, "That isn't fair!"

TWO small sacks of salty snacks.

THREE young yaks with black backpacks.

TWO yaks put snacks in their packs.

ONE mad yak yelps, "Where's *my* snack?"

THREE fast scooters, painted teal.

FOUR ball-bouncing silver seals.

THREE seals steal a set of wheels.

ONE seal gets a real bad deal.

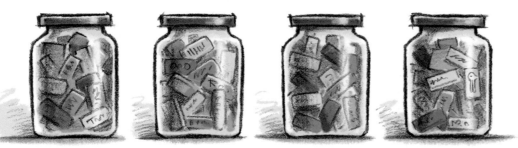

FOUR large jars of candy bars.

Greedy goats in **FIVE** red cars.

FOUR goats gobble all the bars.

ONE goat finds four empty jars.

Pillows sit on FIVE flat mats.

Nap, nap, nap, think SIX fat cats.

FIVE fat cats nap on their mats.

ONE fat cat thinks, Rats! **Rats! Rats!**

SIX cookbooks in narrow nooks.

SEVEN apron-wearing cooks.

SIX cooks pull books out of nooks.

ONE cook gives them grumpy looks.

SEVEN jet skis, shiny blue.

EIGHT cows craving something new.

SEVEN cows call, "Moo woo-hoo!"

ONE hot cow stews, "Moo boo-hoo!"

EIGHT long sticks and one slick puck.

NINE excited skating ducks.

EIGHT ducks play with sticks and puck.

ONE poor duck is out of luck.

NINE trombones, all gold and grand.

WHO WANTS TO LEARN TO PLAY THE TROMBONE?

TEN baboons all raise a hand.

NINE baboons march with the band.

ONE baboon gets less than planned.

TEN tall, twisty playground slides.

TWENTY pigs all want a ride.

"Piggyback!" the pigs decide.

TEN pairs glide down side by side.

Bears can see it's fun to share.

They try sharing underwear!

Seals and yaks soon follow suit,
sharing snack packs while they scoot.

Cows, baboons,

and cats and cooks

share their boats, horns, mats, and books.

Goats and ducks share candy bars,
hockey fun, and empty jars.

The friends all share and swap and trade then line up in a long parade.

How did they learn
to count and share?

From **ONE** big pair of underwear!

The end

For my family, with love—L. G.   For my dad, in loving memory—T. L.

BEACH LANE BOOKS • An imprint of Simon & Schuster Children's Publishing Division • 1230 Avenue of the Americas, New York, New York 10020 • Text copyright © 2014 by Laura Gehl • Illustrations copyright © 2014 by Tom Lichtenheld • All rights reserved, including the right of reproduction in whole or in part in any form. • BEACH LANE BOOKS is a trademark of Simon & Schuster, Inc. • For information about special discounts for bulk purchases, please contact Simon & Schuster Special Sales at 1-866-506-1949 or business@simonandschuster.com. • The Simon & Schuster Speakers Bureau can bring authors to your live event. For more information or to book an event, contact the Simon & Schuster Speakers Bureau at 1-866-248-3049 or visit our website at www.simonspeakers.com. • Book design by Tom Lichtenheld and Lauren Rille • The text for this book is set in Brandon Grotesque. • The illustrations for this book are rendered in pencil, with digital color and assistance from Kristen Cella. • Manufactured in China • 1014 SCP • 10 9 8 7 6 5 4 3 • Library of Congress Cataloging-in-Publication Data • Gehl, Laura. • One big pair of underwear / Laura Gehl wrote the words ; Tom Lichtenheld made the pictures. • pages cm • Summary: Progressively larger groups of animals try to share a limited number of scooters, cookbooks, nap mats, and underwear. • ISBN 978-1-4424-5336-4 (hardcover) — ISBN 978-1-4424-5338-8 (ebook) [1. Stories in rhyme. 2. Sharing—Fiction. 3. Animals—Fiction. 4. Counting.] I. Lichtenheld, Tom, illustrator. II. Title. • PZ8.3.G273On 2014 • [E]—dc23 • 2013041926